THIS BOOK BELONGS TO

LAURA

# Cinderella

# Cinderella

Retold by

P E T E R   E L W E L L

Illustrated by

J A D A   R O W L A N D

A CALICO BOOK

Published by Contemporary Books, Inc.

CHICAGO · NEW YORK

To Sparks

—J.R.

A Calico Book
Published by Contemporary Books, Inc.
180 North Michigan Avenue, Chicago, Illinois 60601
Copyright © 1988 by The Kipling Press
Text Copyright © 1988 by Peter Elwell
Cover Illustrations Copyright © 1988 by Peter Elwell
Illustrations Copyright © 1988 Jada Rowland
All Rights Reserved.

Designed by Gloria Priam
International Standard Book Number: 0-8092-4484-5
Manufactured in the United States of America

Published simultaneously in Canada by Beaverbooks, Ltd.
195 Allstate Parkway, Valleywood Business Park
Markham, Ontario L3R 4T8 Canada

**Library of Congress Cataloging Data**
Elwell, Peter
Cinderella / retold by Peter Elwell;
illustrated by Jada Rowland.
"A Calico book."
Summary: Retells the fairy tale of the mistreated daughter
who wins a better life with a prince through the help
of her fairy godmother.
ISBN 0-8092-4484-5 : $12.95
[1. Fairy tales.    2. Folklore.]    I. Rowland, Jada, ill.
II. Cinderella.    III. Title.
PZ8.E5Ci    1988    88-21982    398.2'1—dc19

# Cinderella

Once upon a time, there was a gentleman who lived in great happiness with his wife and small daughter. Sadly, his wife fell ill and, sadder still, she died. The gentleman grieved bitterly over the loss of his wife, but his heart did not break, for he found both joy and comfort in the child.

In time, his wife became a sweet memory. It seemed proper that he find another wife for himself and a new mother for his daughter, so he met and married a widow—a widow who had two daughters of her own.

As the years passed, the three daughters became young women. The gentleman's daughter grew to look more and more like her mother, and her father could not look at her without being filled with the memory of his first wife. He would become sad and silent, and it didn't take the widow long to figure out why. She hated

the girl who reminded her husband of his first wife, and
soon her daughters took up their mother's dislike for
their stepsister. They did not treat her like a sister at all,
but like a servant, and a poor servant at that. The girl
thought she must have done something wrong to
deserve such treatment, so she bent over backwards to
please her stepsisters and never complained when they
found fault with her every move. She bore their ill will
patiently and with a good temper. In the still of night,
though, she would find herself remembering the mother
who once cradled her tenderly.

Now, in a world where the rusty wheel gets the
grease, this girl was bound to be forgotten by her father,
for her stepsisters were the rustiest wheels there ever
were. They would squeak and stamp for what they
wanted, and what they wanted, they got. As it turned
out, they wanted a lot: the finest mirrors to admire
themselves in, the finest clothes in which to be admired
by others, and the finest beds to sleep in after a busy day
of so much admiration. Nothing was too good for them.
They were, after all, and in their own eyes, fine ladies.
So they had the finest servant, cook, hairdresser,
chambermaid, and housekeeper: their young stepsister.

She lived in a cold attic room and slept on a bed of straw. Her days began and ended in the service of her stepsisters, and she came to believe that it was nothing less than an honor to serve such fine ladies.

It was her habit, after the day's work was done, to sit by the fire in the cinders. One of her stepsisters, in a waggish mood, noticed this and said, "Since you're always covered with ash and cinders, perhaps I'll call you *Cinderella*." There was no "perhaps" about it—that is exactly what she did, and thus the girl came to be known as Cinderella.

In the spring of Cinderella's sixteenth year, the King's son decided to give a grand and glorious ball. It was to be a splendid affair, and everyone who was anyone was invited. "That, of course, means *us*," said one of the stepsisters.

"Not *you*, Cinderella," added the other.

"Why, you've been a drudge so long, you wouldn't know how to act like a proper lady," said their mother. "It's not likely that a prince or duke would marry my girls if he knew they lived in the same house with you."

Cinderella looked down at her ragged clothes and dirty hands and, despite the ache in her heart to go to

the ball, agreed. "I suppose you're right. Besides, I'll have my hands full getting you ready."

Cinderella's hands were full, indeed. The next several days were spent attending to the grand design of making her stepsisters look like proper bait for proper husbands. A king's ransom was spent on their velvet gowns. Their hair was curled and powdered, their faces painted and patched; their bodies were cinched in this way and puffed out that way. The night of the ball finally arrived. On went the ball gowns, along with a bucket of perfume, and off they went. Cinderella had worked long and hard preparing her stepsisters and she'd done the job well; they looked like the finest of fine ladies.

The house was suddenly empty and quiet. Cinderella, left alone, sat down by the fire and, for the first time since her mother died, burst into tears. It wasn't just because she couldn't go to the ball; the silence of the house reminded her of how long it had been since anyone had spoken to her with affection. At that very moment, she heard a voice say, "Why are you sitting there like a lump of coal when there's so much to do?"

Cinderella looked up, wiped the tears from her eyes, and saw a woman standing in the room with her. The woman was pretty and looked strangely familiar. But the most remarkable thing about her was that she had little wings, something Cinderella had never seen before, not even on fine ladies.

"Who are you?" asked Cinderella.

"I'm your Fairy Godmother," the woman replied.

"Now, if you plan to go to the Prince's ball, we'd better get to work."

The Fairy Godmother picked up a mousetrap which was in a corner by the fireplace. The trap had six mice in it, all of them fat and jolly. "Ah, you'll do nicely, my beauties," laughed the Fairy Godmother, and she tripped out into the garden, carrying the mice with her.

"Ah!" exclaimed the Godmother, "Now *that's* a pumpkin!" Saying this, she waved her wand over the pumpkin, and, in a wink, it was changed into a coach —a beautiful, shining coach, covered with gilding and shimmering like the stars.

"Why, it's almost like magic," gasped Cinderella.

"Why, it *is* magic," said her Fairy Godmother. She then opened the mousetrap and, as each mouse scampered out, she waved her wand over them.

One by one, the mice grew into magnificent, milk-white horses, their manes bobbed and their tails knotted into the tidiest Turk's heads. They were the most noble carriage horses Cinderella had ever seen. A rat, startled by the neighing and stamping of these horses, bolted out of hiding and skittered right over the Fairy Godmother's feet. She waved her wand again, and, in a flash, the rat was changed into a coachman. He had long whiskers and wore a coachman's caped coat. In his hand, he carried a whip to crack over the horses' heads.

"Something's missing," muttered the Fairy Godmother. "Aha! You need footmen, my dear."

Over by the water spout, six lizards had been
peering shyly at the odd goings-on. Before they could
make head or tail of the matter, the wand was waved
and—"Ping!"—the lizards were lizards no longer, but
footmen, trimly decked out in footmen's liveries. Four
of them ran and took their places behind the coach,
while the other two, torches in hand, ran to the front of
the carriage to light the way. The coachman turned to
Cinderella and said, "Madam, we await your pleasure."

Cinderella looked at the coachman, the coach,
the horses, and the footmen, and said, "Oh sir . . . oh,
Mister Rat, I can't ride in your beautiful coach. You are

all so spruce and proper; I'd shame you in the rags I wear."

"Madam, rats know no shame," replied the coachman. "Besides, right now, I might *appear* to be a coachman but, as you know, I *am* a rat. You, on the other hand, might appear to be a low sort but, as I know, you are as fine and lovely a lady as any around. To serve you is no shame. It is a great honor."

The lizard footmen added to the rat coachman's speech with a hearty "Hear, hear!"

The Fairy Godmother smiled on her handiwork. Addressing Cinderella, she said, "My dear, I can easily change your clothes, and so I will, but I wouldn't change *you* for the world. You are my godchild. I have watched you and known you these many years and I have loved you for what you are. The time has come for others to do so, too." With that, she waved her wand and Cinderella's rags were transformed into a gown of the richest satin, hung with pearls and spattered with diamonds. Her hair was done up in the most fashionable and elaborate coif, and on her feet were the daintiest slippers, made of glass.

Cinderella, breathless and bewildered, stepped toward the coach. The footmen leapt from their places, opened the carriage door, and, bowing and bobbing, helped her into the coach.

"Remember," said the Fairy Godmother, "what you see here is an enchantment. When the clock strikes midnight, the spell will be over. You, your coach and six, coachman, footmen, and all will return to what you were. Be home before the clock strikes twelve!"

The coachman cracked his whip and the horses were off at a gallop. Looking behind her, Cinderella could no longer see a trace of her Godmother, for the fairy had vanished just as quickly as she had appeared.

When Cinderella's coach appeared before the palace, all the Prince's guests ran out to look at it. "Who could it be?" they wondered. They had never seen such a carriage, such magnificent steeds, such nimble footmen or such a noble coachman. But when Cinderella stepped out of the coach, the "Ooohs!" and "Ahs!" rippled through the crowd and drowned out all other conversation.

Cinderella walked through the admiring throng

and into the Great Ballroom. At the end of the hall stood the Prince. He was elegant and handsome and, being a prince, quite used to having remarkable people in his company. This lady, however—this vision of beauty, this enchantress—was another matter. As she walked toward the Prince, his heart fluttered and, when she curtsied before him, it melted. To him, every move she made was the very picture of grace and perfection.

Cinderella was concerned that the Prince would discover she was not the fine lady she appeared to be. However, when the orchestra struck up the first dance, a

slow and stately sarabande, the Prince, bowing low, said, "Madam, I await your pleasure." Cinderella smiled. "It's funny," she thought, "that a Prince and a rat should say the same thing." And she silently wondered who was the nobler of the two.

Cinderella danced, and danced beautifully. It seemed as if the glass slippers she was wearing actually knew the proper steps to each dance. One of Cinderella's stepsisters was even heard remarking, "I *must* learn to dance like that!"

The Prince was in Cinderella's company the entire

evening. He was utterly enchanted by her conversation, which mostly had to do with cleaning house, step-sisters, rats, mice, and lizards—subjects completely new and fascinating to the Prince. As the evening went merrily on, it soon became apparent that for all intents and purposes, the Prince was quite thoroughly in love.

The hours seemed to fly and, in no time at all, it was just a few minutes to midnight. "Midnight!" Cinderella cried. "Oh, sir, I must go!"

"I beg of you, stay a bit longer . . . ," exclaimed the Prince, but the clock had already begun to ring twelve.

Cinderella, desperate for fear that she'd be found out, pulled away from the Prince, and ran through the ballroom, out the great doors, and down the steps. Just as she was passing through the palace gates, her finery turned to rags. A palace guard, seeing her in her tattered attire, said, "Away from here, beggar. The palace is no place for the likes of you."

Cinderella's horses, coachman, and footmen were nowhere to be found. They had already changed back to their former states and scampered off into the night. The coach was nothing but a pumpkin in the gutter, crushed beneath the wheels of real coaches as they departed in the night. In tears, Cinderella ran down the dark streets towards home. The Prince stood on the palace steps, looking frantically this way and that, asking if anyone had seen a lady of extraordinary beauty. "No, Sire," said the guard, "just a beggar girl."

As the Prince turned back to the palace, he noticed something on the steps: it was one of Cinderella's glass slippers, which had fallen off in her haste to escape before midnight. He gently picked up the slipper and, holding it to his heart, walked sadly back to the ballroom.

Later that night, when Cinderella's stepsisters got home, they were all aflutter about the mysterious lady who had stolen the Prince's heart. "*I* think she's an Indian queen," said one.

"*I* think she's a fairy princess," said the other.

"Whoever she is, she must be very nice," said Cinderella.

The stepsisters agreed that she was very nice indeed—not only nice, but clever and particularly well bred. Then they talked of her dancing—of how perfect and lovely it was, and of how sad the Prince was after she left, and of how he wouldn't dance with anyone else, but chose to spend the rest of the ball mooning over a glass shoe.

Though Cinderella listened to all this with a smile, she couldn't help but feel a trifle sad herself, for she had grown rather fond of the Prince. True, the thought of him mooning over her shoe made him seem a bit silly, but, curiously, it made her like him all the more.

The Prince was a young man with a decidedly romantic streak. The next morning he stayed in bed, claiming to be dying of love. Unless the owner of the glass slipper was found, he was sure he would not be long for this world. The doctors who attended him did not necessarily agree with this diagnosis, but they decided to go along with it anyway. He was, after all, the Prince, and could die from any ailment he chose.

Thus it was that the sound of trumpets and drums rang and rattled through the streets early that morning, announcing the Lord Chamberlain as he went from house to house with the glass slipper, seeking its owner.

Every female over the age of twelve and under the age of ninety tried on that slipper, but to no avail. The shoe fit no one. As the day wore on, the Chamberlain began to mutter unpleasant comments about romantic princes who made their Lord Chamberlains go about the Kingdom trying shoes on strangers.

At last, the Lord Chamberlain arrived at Cinderella's house. The stepsisters wasted neither time nor effort in trying to get the slipper on. They wiggled and writhed and squirmed and squeezed—but it was no use. Finally, one of the stepsisters shouted angrily, "If it's a fine lady you're looking for, maybe you should try the shoe on Cinderella!"

The other sister laughed haughtily at the joke and added, "That is, if you don't mind getting such a pretty little shoe dirty."

The Lord Chamberlain did not seem to mind at all and, to the stepsisters' surprise, asked that Cinderella be sent for as quickly as possible. Cinderella walked shyly up to the Lord Chamberlain and sat down. He knelt to

try the shoe on her foot. When her heel slipped neatly into the glass shoe, the stepsisters were struck dumb in mid-giggle. It fit!

The Lord Chamberlain, however, was at no loss for words. "Send for the Prince! We've found his lady!"

When word reached the Prince, he leapt out of bed and, in a trice, stood at Cinderella's door, demanding that she show herself. Reluctantly, Cinderella came out. The Prince said nothing, but simply looked at her.

"As you can see," said Cinderella, "I am not an Indian queen. I am no fairy princess. I am only what you see before you."

The Prince dropped to his knee and said, "Madam, had you appeared at the ball exactly as you are now, I would have loved you none the less and all the same. I am your servant, to do with as you please."

"Then walk with me in the garden," said Cinderella, taking the Prince's hand. And they walked in the garden.

Not long after, Cinderella and the Prince were married.

Among the guests were, of course, Cinderella's father, stepmother, and stepsisters. Her father, gazing at his daughter with her husband, remarked on how much she looked like her mother on the day of her wedding. Suddenly he grew pale and silent.

"What is it?" asked Cinderella.

Haltingly, her father said, "In trying to forget the pain of my own loss, I succeeded only in forgetting you. I ask your forgiveness."

Cinderella kissed the father she had missed for so long. Her stepmother asked for forgiveness, too, and received it, as did her stepsisters—though, if the truth be told, they were hoping for noble husbands through Cinderella's forgiveness.

Also invited to the wedding was Cinderella's Fairy Godmother. Though Cinderella looked for her among the wedding crowd, she could not find her. When everyone sat down to the feast, a mysterious coachman walked into the feasting hall. The crowd fell silent. Cinderella smiled, for she recognized this coachman. "Ah, Mister Rat," she said. "You are welcome here."

"I thank you, Madam," said the rat coachman, "but my time is brief. I've come only to bring you this little note." With a low bow, a smile, and a wink, the coachman presented Cinderella with a letter.

"It's from my Fairy Godmother!" Cinderella exclaimed, as she eagerly opened it.

This is what the letter said: "My dearest Cinderella. Though I'll always be near you, you will not see me again. Fairy Godmothers can only appear when they're needed, and who needs a Fairy Godmother when they will live happily ever after?"

The Fairy Godmother was right, as Fairy Godmothers always are, for Cinderella and her Prince did, indeed, live happily ever after.